FROGGY
GOES TO
BED

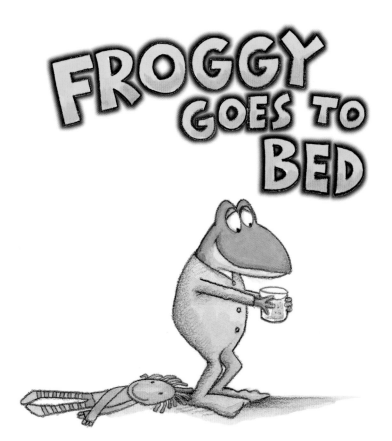

FROGGY GOES TO BED

JONATHAN LONDON

ILLUSTRATED BY
FRANK REMKIEWICZ

RED FOX

For Froggy's mother, Maureen
    —J. L.

For Jessica
    —F. R.

A Red Fox Book

Published by Random House Children's Books
20 Vauxhall Bridge Road, London SW1V 2SA

A division of The Random House Group Ltd
London Melbourne Sydney Auckland
Johannesburg and agencies throughout the world

First published in the United States of America in 2000 by Viking,
a division of Penguin Putnam Books for Young Readers

Red Fox edition 2001

Printed and bound in China

THE RANDOM HOUSE GROUP Limited Reg. No. 954009

www.randomhouse.co.uk

ISBN 978 1 84 941442 5

It was late.
Froggy was too pooped to pop.
He'd been playing hard at Max's all day long.

FRROOGGYY!

called his mother.
"Wha-a-a-t?"
"It's time for bed!"

"No!" cried Froggy.
"I'm not tired."

"Why don't you take
a nice bath?" she said.
"We'll make it a bubble bath."

"Okay," said Froggy. "But first I have to find my boat!" – *flop flop flop*.

He looked in the fridge.
"Nope!"

He looked beneath the sink.
"Not here!"

He looked in the
laundry basket.
"Found it!"

And he took a bath – *splash splash splash.*

"Now it's time to put
your pyjamas on!" said his mother.
And she wrapped him all
cosy warm in a towel.

"Okay," said Froggy. "But first
I have to find them!" – *flop flop flop*.

He looked on his floor.
"Nope!"
He looked in his toy chest. "Not here!"
He looked behind his desk. "Found them!"
And he put them on – *zwoop*.

FRROOGGYY!

called his mother.
"Wha-a-a-t?"
"It's time to brush!" said his mother.

"Okay," said Froggy. "But first
I have to find my toothbrush!" – *flop flop flop*.

He looked in the fishbowl.
Nope.

He looked in the wastepaper basket.
"Not here!"

He looked in the biscuit tin.
"Found it!"

And he brushed his gums – *brush brush brush*.

FRROOGGYY!

called his mother.
"Wha-a-a-t?"
"I bet you want your huggy," said his mother.

"Yep!" said Froggy.
"I have to find my huggy!" – *flop flop flop.*

"Oh, here it is!
It's under the stove!" *Bonk*!
He gave it a hug and climbed into bed.

"Now it's time to sleep!" said his mother,
and gave him a good night kiss.
"Okay," said Froggy.
"But first I need a snack! *Then* I'll go to sleep."
And he hopped out of bed – *flop flop flop.*

Munch scrunch munch.
He ate a bowl of flies . . .

then crawled back into bed.

"Now go to sleep, Froggy!" said his mother.
She was getting a little tired herself.
"Okay," said Froggy. "But I'm *thirsty!*
And you have to close the wardrobe.
And open my door just a crack!
And turn the night-light down just how I like it!
Then I'll go to sleep!"

"Oh fiddlesticks!" said his mother, and got him a glass of water.

"Oops!" cried Froggy,
looking more red in the face than green.
"It spilled!"

"Oh, Froggy," said his mother.
She wiped it up . . .

then got him
another glass of water —
glug glug glug.

Closed the wardrobe – *slam!*

Opened his door
just a crack – *cr-e-eak*.

And turned down
the light just right.
"*Now go to sleep!*" she said.

"Okay," said Froggy. "But first . . .
will you read me a story?"
"Of course, dear." She yawned.

And she read . . .

and she read . . .

and she read . . . till the book dropped –
thump!—
and she fell asleep,
snoring like a horse.

"Good night, Mum," said Froggy.

Then he closed his eyes and went to sleep – zzzzzzzzzz.

"Good night, Froggy!" said Mr Owl, sitting on a branch.

WHO WHO WHOOOOO